THE RAGGED HATMAKER

Victorian Romance

FAYE GODWIN

Tica House Publishing

Sweet Romance that Delights and Enchants!

PERSONAL WORD FROM THE AUTHOR

Dearest Readers,

I'm so delighted that you have chosen one of my books to read. Thank you! I am proud to be a part of the team of writers at Tica House Publishing. Our goal is to inspire, entertain, and give you many hours of reading pleasure. Your kind words and loving readership are deeply appreciated.

I would like to personally invite you to sign up for updates and to become part of our **Exclusive Reader Club**—it's completely Free to Join! I'd love to welcome you!

Much love,

Faye Godwin

VISIT HERE to Join our Reader's Club and to Receive Tica House Updates:

http://ticahousepublishing.subscribemenow.com

PART I

CHAPTER 1

London, England

"FERN, PLEASE COME OUT," A THIN VOICE WAILED.

Fern Hall heard the plaintive cry though the flimsy paneled wooden door of the closet.

She shifted closer to the door. Her back ached from the caning she'd received before she'd been locked in the closet by the matron of the Home for Indigent Girls.

"I can't come out right now, Pearl," she whispered with her face pressed close to the barrier separating her from the little girl. Fern wouldn't be let out until she was prepared to repent for her supposed misdeeds. She'd stubbornly held out for hours already, and Pearl had obviously noticed her absence.

"You need to go. You'll get in trouble if Matron finds you here."

The thought of Pearl's thin, frail body suffering any sort of punishment was much worse than the pain of Fern's bruised back.

Pearl rattled the doorknob. "Why can't you come out?"

Fern couldn't tell Pearl the truth, that Matron was punishing her for stealing extra food from the morning meal to give to Pearl. Though Fern couldn't see Pearl right now, she could picture the little girl in her mind; her hollowed cheeks, her tiny body that looked like that of a four-year-old, though Pearl had already seen six years. The little girl was so pale and sickly. Fern feared what would happen to her, even now that she had been taken off the filthy streets and brought into the comparative safety of the Home after a year of surviving on her own. Though in truth, the orphanage seemed little better at times.

Fern could hear Pearl's sobs, but she was unable to reach the little girl to offer her comfort.

"You must be quiet, Pearl, or Matron will hear you and punish you," Fern warned.

"I want you out here with me," Pearl choked out between sniffles.

Fern didn't know how to reply. She had no words to sooth the little girl's upset. Pulling her knees up to her chest, Fern wrapped her arms around her bent legs. Her foot bumped against something in the dark.

The closet was a tiny space, barely large enough for Fern to sit on the hard, wooden floor amid the clutter of dirty brooms, mops, and feather dusters. The only meager bit of light came from the crack around the door, but it did nothing to chase away the darkness. Though Fern couldn't see them, she knew there were cobwebs in the corners of the closet. Imagining a giant spider coming down to crawl across her skin, she couldn't repress a slight shudder. If she could see the spiders, they didn't bother her. But something about not knowing what might be coming or when it might happen, had her feeling on edge.

Fern had come to the orphanage when she was ten, after her mother had abandoned her in a market one day. The Home's matron had come upon her, and Fern had believed it a stroke of good fortune.

She hadn't known that she would be treated little better than unpaid labor, expected to work from dawn till dusk with hardly a break in between. Pearl was made to endure such an existence as well, despite her frail health.

Fern shuddered. The other girls who would pick on Pearl, if Fern wasn't there to put a stop to it. Who would protect Pearl while she was locked inside here? She had to get out so she could keep Pearl safe.

But she wasn't truly sorry for what she'd done. Pearl would

never get well without proper nourishment, especially since she was not allowed the rest which would have surely brought an improvement to her health.

Fern would have to pretend she had seen the error of her ways, though she knew she'd do the very same thing again without hesitation.

For three years, Matron had tried to cow Fern into meekness and obedience by canings and locking her in the closet—for even the most minor infraction of the Home's rules. But the older woman hadn't succeeded yet in breaking Fern's spirit.

Just then, Fern heard heavy footsteps in the corridor.

"Go, Pearl!" she hissed, then listened to the sound of Pearl's running feet.

A moment later, the heavy footsteps stopped outside the closet door. A key rattled in the lock, and then the door was pulled open. Fern put up a hand to shield her eyes as the sudden brightness blinded her.

When her eyes adjusted, she saw Matron silhouetted in the doorway, backlit by the spattering of sunlight coming in the soot-covered window on the wall behind her. The woman wore a starched high-neck dress of dull brown wool, her gray-streaked black hair pulled into a severe bun at her nape.

Her face was in the shadows, making it impossible for Fern to read her expression. But she knew Matron well enough to picture the scowl on her thin lips and her dark eyebrows pinched together in a fierce glower meant to intimidate and frighten unruly little girls.

It didn't work on Fern, however. She pushed to her feet, her back protesting the movement, though she was determined not to show it.

"Do you have anything to say for yourself, girl?" Matron demanded.

Fern lowered her gaze, hoping she looked suitably humbled and repentant. "I'm very sorry for what I did, Matron."

"Are you? We shall see. The punishment will be much more severe if you are caught stealing again."

Fern kept her eyes downcast, not wanting to risk giving away her true feelings. Threats of punishment did not frighten her. "Yes, Matron."

"And there will be no more sneaking Pearl into your bed at night."

Fern's head jerked up.

"Yes, I know about that, too. I know everything that goes on here. And it is at an end now. Or Pearl will receive the same punishment as you."

"But—"

"Do I need to return you to the closet right now?"

"No, Matron." She dipped her chin down to hide her defiant expression.

It caused a sharp pain in Fern's heart to think of Pearl crying herself to sleep, for that was what had happened when Pearl had first come to the Home. But now, Matron would ensure she no longer brought Pearl into her own bed at night to sooth the little girl's fears. The older woman did not make idle threats.

Matron gave a sharp nod at Fern's reply. "Good. Now return to your chores in the kitchen at once. After you finish helping prepare the meal, you will wash and scrub every pot and pan by yourself. There will be no supper for you until the room is spotless."

"Yes, Matron."

As Fern walked away, she heard the older woman mutter under her breath.

"I'll beat that red-headed temper out of you yet, girl. Just see if I don't."

Fern wasn't sure if Matron had intended her to hear it or not, but she rather suspected the former, since the older woman had said those words directly to Fern countless times before. She no longer paid them any mind.

After she reached the kitchen, she spent hours peeling potatoes for the evening meal. Bending over the pile of peelings did nothing to lessen the pain in her back, but she did her best to ignore it.

The moment she was granted a few moments to herself to visit the privy, she veered toward the back stairs and snuck up them to check on Pearl instead.

Fern needed to explain to her that she wouldn't be able to sneak Pearl into her bed at night any more, but she dreaded the little girl's reaction. No matter how she pleaded and cried, Fern could not give in, however. Not with the threat of punishment over Pearl's head, too.

She entered the dormitory tucked under the steep-pitched rafters. She found Pearl helping several other girls wash the streaked windows.

Weak light streamed into the dim room filled with rows of narrow beds lining two walls, and a thin walkway down the middle. The bedding was shabby and threadbare, inadequate to keep out the chill at night. The floorboards underfoot were worn down from years of girls scrubbing the wide planks with rough brushes. And the walls were a dingy gray from the soot that seemed to hang in the air as a haze over this dismal and dangerous area of the city. It coated every surface, never allowing them to get anything truly clean, no matter how many hours they labored at their tasks.

A girl a year younger than Fern's own age of three and ten turned around, a superior expression twisting her freckled face into an unattractive mask as she caught sight of Fern. "You're not supposed to be here. I'm going to tell Matron."

"If you do, you'll regret it." Fern gave her a fierce glare. "Remember what happened last time?"

The other girl paled, losing her spiteful smirk as her hand went to the short, hacked ends of her lank brown hair.

Pearl came running up to Fern and wrapped her thin arms around her waist, pressing herself close.

"And I better not hear you've been bothering Pearl again either." Fern shifted a narrow-eyed glance to the other girls who had stopped their work to watch the confrontation between Fern and Edwina. "That goes for all of you," she warned.

They gave frightened nods and hastily turned back to their work, not wanting to be the focus of Fern's attention.

She nodded in satisfaction. While some of the other girls seemed to take great delight in tattling to Matron, Fern preferred to get even. Though no one wanted to admit it, they all feared what Fern might do to them when her red-headed temper was riled.

A spider in their porridge, a rat in their bed, their hair hacked off with sewing shears—Edwina wasn't the only one who had been on the receiving end of Fern's retribution. It was no less than they deserved for their cruel acts toward Pearl or any of the other girls who were younger than them.

Of course, Fern was always punished for her actions but that never stopped her, and so the other girls were wary. None of them had anything to fear from her, however, as long as they were kind.

When Fern told Pearl what she'd come to say, the little girl clung to her all the tighter. Though Pearl's protests pierced Fern's heart, she couldn't allow them to sway her.

At last, she forced herself to step back from the little girl. "I have to get back to the kitchen before Matron comes looking for me."

"No, don't go!" Pearl latched on to her hand in a bid to keep Fern there. Tears rolled down her thin cheeks, leaving tracks in the dirt smudged on her pale skin.

"I have to, Pearl." Fern hated that she had no other choice.

She pulled Pearl close again for a moment, hugging the little girl tightly to her and stroking the tangled locks of Pearl's dull blond hair. "I'll come visit you again when I can," she promised.

Putting the little girl away from her, Fern turned, unable to look at Pearl's brown eyes filled with tears.

As Fern walked out of the dormitory, Pearl continued to sob behind her, and the sound nearly broke Fern's heart. But she didn't turn back. She couldn't. Because then she might not be able to leave the little girl, and when Matron caught them together, Fern wouldn't be the only one to pay the price. Fern didn't fear punishment for herself, but little Pearl's fragile health might not survive a beating or meals being withheld. She was sickly enough as it was, being made to work without rest.

Fern hoped Pearl would be adopted and taken away from all this. That she would have a peaceful life with caring parents, abundant food on the table, and no need to spend hours on backbreaking work. She was young enough—there was still a chance for her.

But for Fern, there was no way out.

CHAPTER 2

After that day, Fern tried to avoid any infractions that would lead to a return to the broom closet. She didn't want to leave Pearl on her own again. The older girls might take advantage of the opportunity to pick on her while Fern was locked away and unable to come to her defense. Though Fern hated that she could no longer bring Pearl into her bed at night to comfort the little girl, she didn't dare defy Matron for fear that Pearl might be punished—or that Fern's punishment would take her away from the younger girl completely.

She managed to steal quick visits to check on Pearl during the day, but she was only able to see her for a moment or two before she was forced to return to her own chores. She couldn't risk any more than that—she couldn't bear the thought that she might be the cause of Pearl suffering harsh consequences.

Still, she struggled to rein in her defiant nature, with much less success on some occasions than on others. Although she didn't try to sneak any extra food to Pearl, Fern could not meekly stand by and do nothing against deliberate acts of cruelty by some of the older girls. This meant she did not escape punishment entirely for her supposed misdeeds, of which there were many, according to Matron.

But she was careful not to get caught doing anything that would warrant Matron locking her in that tiny closet once more.

Over the next several weeks, she was allowed little time with Pearl, apart from at meals. Then, one dreary winter's morning, she noticed that Pearl seemed to have developed a terrible cough. When Fern looked closer at the little girl, she noticed that Pearl appeared even thinner and paler than before.

Concern filled her. "Pearl, what's the matter?"

The little girl looked up at her with a glassy-eyed gaze. "I don't feel well."

"Is it just a cough?" Fern asked, though she feared it was much worse than that.

The little girl shook her head, but didn't offer anything more.

Fern lifted her hand to feel Pearl's brow and found her skin burning up with fever. "Let's get you tucked back into bed."

She steered Pearl toward the dormitory even as the little girl started to protest.

"I have chores to do. Matron will punish me if they aren't done." Fear filled her big brown eyes at the prospect.

Fern recognized the truth in her words, but Pearl was in no condition to lug heavy buckets of water and scrub the wooden floors. "I'll do them for you," she promised as she urged the younger girl under the blanket. "You just rest for now."

Pearl offered little resistance. As soon as she'd laid down, she heaved a weary sigh and closed her eyes. Fern watched her for a handful of seconds, wishing a doctor could be sent for, but knowing that Matron would never allow it. The older woman refused to take heed unless someone was quite literally at death's door. Fern couldn't remember the last time the doctor had come to the orphanage to attend to one of the girls.

A creeping feeling of dread spread inside Fern at the little girl's waxen complexion, and she feared that Pearl might not get better. Resolutely, she banished her grim thoughts before they could torment her further.

"I'll come back to check on you soon," Fern whispered before she left the room to tackle her own chores and Pearl's as well.

Of course, it wasn't long before Matron found out Pearl had taken to her bed. And she was far from sympathetic toward the little girl's illness. She discovered that Fern was frequently hovering at Pearl's bedside, determined to protect her.

"Why is she in bed in the middle of the day?" the older woman demanded. She didn't allow Fern a chance to respond before she turned her hard gaze to Pearl. "Get up at once!"

Fern laid her hand on the little girl's arm to keep her from scurrying to do the older woman's bidding. "Pearl's sick, Matron."

"That's no excuse for laying abed. Every girl here must earn her keep. There are chores to be done. Get out of that bed at once!" She flung the blanket off and reached for Pearl.

Fern inserted herself between the two of them before the older woman could succeed in pulling Pearl from the bed. "She can't do her chores. You've worked her so hard that she's become ill."

Matron focused a steely glare on Fern. "Backtalk like that will earn you another caning," she warned ominously.

But Fern refused to back down. "If you force her to work, she'll only get worse. Pearl needs rest and someone to tend to her."

"And who here do you imagine has time for that?"

"I'll do it," Fern replied without hesitation.

Just as quickly, the older woman shook her head. "There's too much work to be done to spare anyone to nurse an invalid."

"But if Pearl doesn't get well again as soon as can be, other girls might become ill, too. Then who will do all the chores?

And who will you hire out to bring money into the orphanage?" Fern added, knowing that the oldest girls were often sent out to work as maids in the homes of wealthy Londoners.

The girls received a wage for their work, but the moment they returned to the Home at the end of the day, Matron demanded that they hand over to her every single coin they'd earned.

The older woman pursed her thin lips, her eyes narrowing at Fern. "If I allow you to tend to her, I still expect that your chores—and hers—will be done."

Fern bobbed her head in quick agreement, relieved that Matron had been willing to make even that small concession. But she should have known that the older woman would never have given in so easily unless it furthered her own end. One that would no doubt bode ill for Fern.

Despite the sudden sense of foreboding that filled her, Fern refused to fidget under the older woman's hard-eyed stare.

"I also expect to get no more trouble from you. You will do exactly as you're told, without complaint or argument. Is that understood?"

Fern hesitated for a long moment. Many of Matron's rules were cruel and unfair, and Fern knew it would be almost impossible for her to hold her tongue while going meekly along with the older woman's dictates. But for Pearl's sake, she would do it. Fern had no choice if she wanted to be allowed to care for the little girl until she was well again.

"Yes, Matron," Fern agreed, even though she felt like she had just made a bargain with the devil.

This feeling was not diminished by the self-satisfied smile that stretched across the older woman's thin lips. "Good. Now after you finish scrubbing the floors, do not forget that supper is to be served at precisely six o'clock. I will suffer no excuses for even one moment of tardiness."

Fern gave a curt nod in acknowledgement, and the air gusted out of her in relief when Matron departed once more.

Fern slumped down on the bedside next to the younger girl for a moment, but then she quickly stiffened her spine. "There, you see, Pearl, Matron isn't going to punish you."

Pearl offered her a wane smile, but didn't speak. Fern's worry over Pearl increased, and she fetched a bowl of cool water and a rough scrap of cloth to bath the younger girl's fevered brow.

But Fern couldn't stay with Pearl for long before she was forced to leave to complete her chores for the day and to make sure supper would be ready on time. She hesitated for a moment as she stroked her hand over the strands of Pearl's damp blond hair. The little girl seemed to have slipped into a restless slumber.

"I'll be back as soon as I can," Fern promised, though Pearl likely didn't hear her.

Later that night, Fern returned to Pearl's bedside.

"I brought your supper. And look, here's an extra wedge of fresh baked bread." Fern held out the plate of food, pasting a falsely bright smile on her face.

She didn't tell Pearl that the bread was from her own plate since she dared not risk stealing extra helpings for Pearl beyond the small amount allotted to each girl.

Pearl didn't reach for the plate, but only lay listlessly in the bed. "I'm not hungry."

Fern struggled not to let her smile slip, but it was no use. "Please, try to eat a little. You need to eat something so you can get well. Then, it's certain that some nice couple will want to adopt you." She tried to force a note of cheer into her tone, but she feared she'd failed miserably.

Tears suddenly welled in Pearl's brown eyes, her hand grabbing weakly onto the sleeve of Fern's gown. "I don't want to leave you, Fern."

Fern laid her hand over Pearl's smaller one. "Surely, you don't want to stay here?"

Pearl shook her head. "Can't you come with me? Maybe a nice couple will want you, too." A spark of hope filled her gaze.

Fern didn't have the heart to crush that small bit of optimism with the harsh truth. "Perhaps," she agreed, though she knew it was not to be.

She was far too old to be adopted by anybody. But Pearl wasn't —and Fern would never do anything that might risk snatching that hope away from the little girl.

"I remember when a couple visited the Home and adopted Molly Browne, a short time before you came here. She was so happy as she departed, holding her new mother's hand." In truth, Molly had looked apprehensive, plainly scared to leave the only home she'd known over the past three years.

But Fern didn't mention that to Pearl. She hoped that Pearl would be adopted and didn't want the little girl to fear what might happen after she left the orphanage.

She thought of Molly who—with her raven-colored ringlets, rosy round cheeks, and smattering of freckles across her nose —was a few years older than Pearl. Somebody had chosen her, out of all the other girls at the Home for Indigent Girls. So, someone would surely want adorable, little Pearl, who looked younger than her true age and reminded Fern of a fragile porcelain doll.

Fern forced another bright smile to her lips. "I bet Molly has a warm bed to sleep in with plenty of thick blankets. And mountains of food on the table to fill her belly. Maybe there are even other children for her to play with. Doesn't the sound wonderful?"

"Only if you're there, too. I don't want to go without you, Fern."

Fern's heart broke at the tears glistening in Pearl's eyes, but she had to be strong. She had to do what was best for Pearl no matter the pain it caused herself.

No matter how much she would miss Pearl, Fern couldn't be selfish and wish for Pearl to remain here with her. She prayed for Pearl to escape this grim place, for her to live a happy life, far away from here. Surely that was not a great deal to ask.

But Pearl had to get better first. No one wanted to adopt a sickly child.

Fern spooned up a bite of food and held it near Pearl's lips, her own lips firming into an unyielding line. "Your supper's going to get cold if you don't eat it soon. And we don't want Matron to become angry that we let this food go to waste."

The little girl's eyes widened as she shook her head, and then she opened her mouth for the first bite. But she tried to turn her face away after only a few small mouthfuls.

It took a good bit of encouragement and prodding, but finally, Pearl had eaten enough to satisfy Fern.

Placing a kiss on Pearl's overly-warm forehead, Fern sat with the younger girl until she fell asleep.

"I love you, Pearl," she whispered so softly that no one else could hear it.

CHAPTER 3

Countless times over the course of the next week, Fern had to bite her tongue or turn a blind eye to the unkind deeds of some of the other girls. But it was worth it to see Pearl slowly improving. However, though Fern's hands were tied at the moment, it wouldn't always be so. She made note of every cruel taunt and slight by Edwina, and all of the others that went unchecked, vowing to exact justice once Pearl was completely well again and would not suffer for Fern's actions.

The time of reckoning would come. But not quite yet.

"Just you wait, though," she warned softly under her breath, so the other girls wouldn't hear and tattle on her to Matron.

Fern continued to give Pearl a portion of her own supper each day. She gave her every bit of food she could spare and still keep up enough strength to take care of the little girl and complete both their lists of assigned chores.

Though Fern's stomach gnawed with hunger, it was a small price to pay to see Pearl get better.

Fern was a bit surprised that she herself hadn't succumbed to illness from overwork and lack of food and sleep. But she supposed she was too stubborn to yield to any sort of weakness. Mainly because she knew there would be no one to look after Pearl, if anything happened to her.

A few days later, Pearl was well enough to join Fern and the other girls at the table for supper. Although they were not seated close to each other, Fern could see that Pearl looked so much better. Her brown eyes were clear, and there was a bit of color in her thin cheeks.

Fern's lips curved up in a smile at the sight, and when she caught Pearl's gaze, the little girl offered a sweet smile in return. Her brief light and happy mood deflated somewhat, however, when she realized that Matron would expect Pearl to return to work the very next morning. Fern feared that the little girl might suffer a sudden reversal.

She prayed harder than ever that someone would come to the Home and want to adopt the little girl. That a kindly couple would fall in love with Pearl and take her far from the filth and despair of this miserable corner of London.

At breakfast the following day, Matron walked into the dining hall and clapped her hands together to gain everyone's attention. "Girls, we are to have visitors at the Home today, so I expect that every one of you will be on your best behavior—or you will suffer the consequences."

"Yes, Matron," they chorused.

Matron's gaze settled on Fern for a long moment, as though she felt it necessary to issue her a personal warning against causing any trouble. Fern met her stare directly, refusing to cower or lower her eyes in a false show of meekness. The older woman's mouth tightened into a thin line at Fern's defiance, but she didn't say anything more and she turned on her heel and walked out of the room.

Fern wondered if the visitors were gents or ladies who were considering donating a sum of money to help fund the Home. Or would it be a couple who was looking to adopt a child? She hoped for the latter. And hoped even more that they might choose Pearl.

She knew that such speculation was pointless, however. She'd find out soon enough, and until then, she had chores to do. Best not to anger Matron unnecessarily. Fern has done quite enough of that already, and it wouldn't be prudent to try to push her luck any further.

It was several hours later before she had an opportunity to check on Pearl and ensure that she wasn't working too hard, at the risk of her health. If that was the case, Fern intended to put a stop to it at once—never mind what Matron might have to say about it.

But when Fern went in search of the little girl, she couldn't find Pearl anywhere.

Where was she? Had something happened to her? She had seemed to be much better, no longer plagued by the illness that had been brought on by months of ceaseless work and malnourishment. But...had she taken a turn for the worse? What else could it be? Though Fern didn't know the answer, she knew she wouldn't find it here in this empty room.

No matter the stark fear suddenly filling her, Fern had to return to her abandoned chores in the kitchen. She'd likely been gone too long as it was, and Matron might have already noted her absence.

Fern didn't encounter the older woman as she made her way back down the stairs. She breathed a tiny sigh of relief when she entered the kitchen and Matron wasn't waiting there for her to mete out punishment.

Despite that small bit of luck, a much greater worry still weighed on Fern. What had become of Pearl?

"Do you know where Pearl is?" she asked one of the other girls working in the kitchen.

"I heard that the couple who came to the orphanage earlier today took her away with them."

"Pearl was adopted?" Fern was stunned. Although she had prayed for this very thing, she hadn't truly believed it would happen.

The couple must have been the visitors that Matron spoke of this morning. Fern had almost forgotten about their expected arrival, since no strangers had appeared in the kitchen while she was busy scrubbing pot and pans and chopping vegetables for a stew.

The other girl shrugged her thin shoulders in response to Fern's question. "I guess so."

Fern mourned the fact that she hadn't gotten the chance to say goodbye to Pearl. But Pearl was in much-improved circumstances now. And Fern could only be happy about that. She hoped Pearl hadn't been too upset at being separated from her so abruptly.

She hated to think that Pearl would continue to cry herself to sleep at night—and Fern wouldn't be there to comfort her. Hopefully, Pearl now had a caring mother to hold her close and dry her tears when the little girl was feeling sad or scared.

Before Fern fell asleep that night, she lay in bed underneath her thin blanket, imagining the wonderful life Pearl would have with a family to love her. No matter that she was stuck here and would miss the younger girl dreadfully, joy filled her heart that Pearl had escaped the grim existence of those still living at the orphanage.

She dreamed of Pearl and her new family—a loving mother and a tenderhearted father, maybe even a cute little terrier as a pet. They would reside in a modest but homey apartment in a respectable section of town—with a fire crackling in the hearth, chasing away the chill in the air, and enough scrumptious-smelling food on the table to fill all their bellies.

The dreary gray light of approaching dawn was a disheartening contrast for Fern when she awoke the next morning. But at least Pearl was warm and comfortable. Fern now imagined the little girl still snuggled up in a soft, cozy bed. That thought lifted her spirits considerably as she climbed out of her own uncomfortable and cold bed. She changed from her thin nightshift into a threadbare cotton dress before heading down to the kitchen to begin the day's work.

IT WAS ONLY A FEW DAYS AFTER PEARL HAD LEFT THAT FERN entered the dining hall for supper and stopped short when she saw Molly Browne sitting on one of the wooden benches lining the long table.

"What are you doing here, Molly?" Fern asked, unable to keep the shock from her voice.

"The Brunners sent me back." Molly fiddled with the edge of her sleeve for a moment then tugged down the frayed fabric to cover her hand.

But not before Fern had seen the purplish bruise that encircled the younger girl's thin wrist.

"What—" Fern cut herself off as Matron appeared unexpectedly in the doorway to the dining hall.

Fern wanted to ask Molly what had happened to her, but Matron's presence prevented it. Despite her unanswered questions—or maybe because of them—a sense of dread filled Fern as she began to imagine one possible explanation after another, each one more horrible than the last.

All through supper, anxiety clawed at her stomach, making it impossible to eat, and she merely pushed the food around on her plate.

It wasn't until much later that night, after the girls were in their beds in the dormitory, that Fern finally learned the truth. And it was every bit as horrific as the worst of her imaginings.

"It was worse living with them than living here," Molly revealed after relaying the grim details of the months of mistreatment and neglect she'd endured at the hands of Mr. and Mrs. Brunner and their hateful children before being sent back to the orphanage.

Her tales of enforced servitude to a family who had claimed to want her as their daughter sent a chill down Fern's spine. Everything the Brunners had said was a lie. They hadn't wanted a daughter. They'd wanted an unpaid servant who had no recourse but to suffer their abuses. It was a wonder that they'd allowed Molly to return. When questioned about their reasons, Molly didn't have an answer.

Fern would certainly never understand why cruel people acted the way they did. And clearly, a person's malicious nature and intentions were not always easily discerned until after it was already too late.

Fern had badly wanted to believe that Pearl was now enjoying a wonderful new life. But had she only been deluding herself? Would they treat her like a beloved daughter? Or was that nothing more than an impossible dream? Fern wanted it to be true, but...

Was Pearl all right? Or was she suffering with no one there to protect her and care for her? Fern hated that she had no way of knowing the answer. That she had no means to find out Pearl's true fate.

The little girl hadn't even been gone a week, but much could happen in that short length of time. Would Pearl end up right back at the orphanage? Or would she be subjected to even worse cruelties at the hands of that unknown couple than anything Matron might have meted out as punishment for a supposed misdeed?

Was there any hope left at all that Pearl would be happy with the strangers who had taken her away? Fern prayed it was so. But bitter experience had taught her that the truth wasn't ever as kind as one might wish. At least, not for people like

Fern, with no family or money—or a true home, since the Home for Indigent Girls was as far from that as it was possible to be.

Life seemed entirely bleak for Fern now, devoid of the merest glimpse of sweet Pearl to lift her spirits and lighten the grim situation at the orphanage—and without even the small speck of joy that she had found in thinking Pearl was in a place far, far better than here.

PART II

CHAPTER 4

Three Years Later

"I'LL BE TAKING THE COST OF THAT TEACUP OUT OF YOUR wages!"

"I'm sorry, Mrs. Phipps. It was an accident," Fern said as she knelt down to gather the shards of broken china covered in soapsuds. "The teacup slipped from my grasp while I was washing it."

"Useless, clumsy maids will receive no pay from me," the older woman continued, ignoring Fern's words of apology.

Surely, the cost of one teacup couldn't equal an entire day's pay. Could it? Given the costly appearance of all the items in this home, perhaps it did. The thought left a sick feeling in the pit of Fern's stomach, as she disposed of the shattered remains of china decorated with hand-painted blue roses.

She took a deep breath in a bid to calm the sudden churning in her middle and turned back to the stacks of dirty dishes still awaiting her on the table next to the basin. Behind her, she heard the housekeeper march out of the kitchen.

She plunged her hands into the soapy water once more and tried not to think about Matron's reaction if Fern returned to the Home later today without the expected coins.

Over the past year, Fern had been sent out to work in the townhouses of wealthy Londoners, including the Hawk Family. Fern was treated with varying degrees of disdain by the upper servants of the fine homes, but Mrs. Phipps was the worst, by far. The older woman looked on Fern with contempt and suspicion because of her lowly origins. Mrs. Phipps had not been shy in expressing the opinion that most orphans were known to be thieves and liars. Fern felt a renewed flush of embarrassment heating her cheeks as she remembered the older woman voicing such sentiments in front of the cook and scullery maids employed by the Hawk Family. The only reason that the housekeeper suffered through Fern's presence here was because Mrs. Hawk was hosting a ball at the end of the coming week and additional help was needed to complete the multitude of preparations.

A short time later, with all her tasks complete, Fern went in search of Mrs. Phipps, though she wasn't looking forward to another confrontation with the housekeeper.

Walking from room to room in the public areas of the town-house, Fern was struck anew by the rich-looking fabrics on the walls, the costly marble floors in the foyer, and intricately carved wooden furniture that was polished to a gleaming shine. Gaslights burned brightly even during the daytime, and copper piping provided water to the kitchen, as well as a bathing chamber and water closet upstairs, though Fern hadn't been privileged enough to set foot in the either of the latter two.

The opulence of the Hawks' London residence was unlike anything she'd ever seen before, even in the other fine homes where she'd worked briefly. The Hawks weren't even members of the nobility, but rather a family of wealthy merchants. Nonetheless, Fern suspected that this mansion would prove unrivaled amongst the highest-ranking lords and ladies of society.

There were expensive Chinese vases, delicate porcelain figurines, and antique curiosities decorating every flat surface. It all looked a bit cluttered to Fern, but it provided the maids with no end of things to clean and dust.

Given the vast number of objects that could be broken or damaged, Fern felt a measure of relief that her duties here had been confined to the kitchen only, thus far. She shuddered to think what Mrs. Phipps would demand in repayment, if Fern had the grave misfortune to cause harm to any of the more costly furnishings or ornamentations on display.

Finding the housekeeper in the front parlor, Fern squared her shoulders as she approached the older woman.

"Mrs. Phipps, I've finished my tasks for the day. May I have my wages before I leave?"

The housekeeper's lips pursed in annoyance, but she nodded her head curtly. "Come with me."

Fern followed the housekeeper through the house to her room near the kitchen, where Mrs. Phipps retrieved a draw-string purse from the small desk positioned against one wall.

The older woman counted out a few coins into Fern's palm, and then tucked the purse away once more. Fern looked down at the coins in her hand, a meager sum much smaller than that which she'd been promised for her work.

She opened her mouth to voice a protest, but before she could get any words out Mrs. Phipps own voice cut across her, obviously guessing Fern's intention to object the paltry amount she's received.

"I shouldn't give you even that much. Be grateful that you got anything at all after breaking the teacup. I expect there will be no more similar incidents before Mrs. Hawk's ball, or I shall have to find another girl to fill the position. I have no use for a maid that can't complete even the simplest of tasks properly."

Though it felt entirely unfair to meekly accept Mrs. Phipps' judgment, Fern knew that trying to argue would do her no good. She had to return to this house tomorrow to work, and for several days afterward, so silence seemed like the better part of valor on this occasion. No matter that biting her tongue was not in Fern's nature.

Pressing her lips tightly closed on any unwise words that would only serve to make the situation worse for herself, she curled her fingers into a fist around the coins.

The housekeeper turned her back to Fern, a clear dismissal. Fern left the room without a word of farewell to the older woman, her gaze directed downward as she tucked the coins into her pocket.

When she lifted her head, she found a person directly in front of her in the hallway, and very narrowly avoided crashing into him.

He was a handsome, young man who looked to be only three or four years older than she. He towered over her, but strangely, his size didn't feel daunting. Short, dark curls framed his clean-shaven face, and his eyes were a warm brown hue flecked with bits of gold and copper.

Pulling up short, Fern dipped into a hasty curtsey. "I beg your pardon, sir," she apologized before stepping around him to continue on her way.

Though she longed to look back at him, she resisted the urge.

But she couldn't help wondering about his identity. His clothing was too fine to be a servant or deliveryman. Was he a tradesman of some sort seeking out Mrs. Phipps to settle his bill? But wouldn't he direct any such inquiries to Mr. Hawk, rather than the housekeeper? Fern had to admit that she knew little regarding the running of a large and grand house.

Not that she expected she would ever have need of that sort of knowledge. She would never be mistress of a fine townhouse like this one. If she married at all, it would be to a man of modest means, someone such as the tradesman behind her, perhaps. She could not hope to rise above that of the wife of a baker or a cobbler. And even that humble elevation in station might prove to be too far beyond the reach of a penniless orphan.

Yet, Fern couldn't deny the fervent wish suddenly filling her heart, that she might know just such a life.

She could still feel the unknown man's gaze upon her as she turned the corner and returned to the kitchen to collect her things before making her way toward the back door which served as the servants' entrance.

GERARD HAWK WATCHED THE YOUNG WOMAN WITH BRIGHT red hair disappear from sight, wishing that she might have stayed long enough for them to exchange a few words— though he wasn't quite sure what had prompted the feeling.

He didn't recognize her as a member of his parents' household staff. From the little bit he had overheard a moment ago, he assumed that she'd been hired as temporary help to aid in preparations for his mother's upcoming ball. Which recalled him to his purpose in seeking out the housekeeper.

Yet, his thoughts turned back to the one-sided conversation that had taken place between the girl and Mrs. Phipps, rather than the matter at hand. He stepped into the doorway leading to the housekeeper's room and cleared his throat to gain the older woman's attention.

She started at the sound and turned to face him, her eyes widening in surprise at his sudden appearance in the servants' quarters. "Oh, Mr. Gerard. I didn't see you standing there." She quickly regained her composure. "Is there something I might do to assist you?"

There was no denying the fact that he wanted to know more about a certain red-haired young woman and her situation, so he didn't try to fight the odd compulsion. "Who was that girl?"

Mrs. Phipps looked at him with a blank expression. "What girl?"

Gerard had never thought the housekeeper was slow-witted, but perhaps he had been mistaken. "The girl who was just here. I passed her in the hall as she left."

The older woman waved her hand in the air as though

shooing away an insignificant gnat. "She's a mere servant, no one of any concern. Fern something or other. I don't recall her full name."

And plainly, the housekeeper was of the opinion that it wasn't important enough for her to bother with remembering the girl's surname.

"An incompetent chit who was hired to help with Mrs. Hawk's ball." Mrs. Phipps barely paused for breath before continuing her diatribe without any prompting from Gerard. "But I don't know that we might be better off without her sort of help. She broke a piece of Mrs. Hawk's best china. I had to take the cost of the teacup out of the girl's wages."

He could scarcely credit that she had said those words with not one single drop of remorse, seemingly unconcerned with the fact that the decrease in wages could mean the difference between having food to eat that day or not.

"Who gave you leave to force this sort of repayment from a servant—and a temporary one, at that?" he questioned, making no attempt to hide his displeasure.

Mrs. Phipps seemed to grow just the slightest bit wary at his harsh tone, but not so much that it stole her voice. "It was never discussed directly, but Mrs. Hawk has always left it to me to deal with the unpleasant business of disciplining the lower members of the household staff when necessary, including those whose employment is of a short duration," she defended her actions.

Gerard wanted to demand that she cease this sort of ill treat-ment at once, even if another item—or a dozen items—should happen to meet a similar fate at Fern's hands. But he didn't feel he could issue instructions to the housekeeper without his mother's knowledge or consent. However, he intended to bring up the matter to her at the first available opportunity.

Would his mother take kindly to Gerard meddling in the running of the household? Or applaud Mrs. Phipps for her shrewd management of the staff and reducing the expenditure required to pay the servants' wages?

The cost of one teacup was insignificant to a family with wealth such as the Hawks, but although his mother had come from a well-to-do family and her father had made a comfort-able income, she was tight-fisted with money. As long as it did not restrict her own luxurious lifestyle, certainly, to which she had grown accustomed since her marriage to Gerard's father, William Hawk.

Of course, she was more than willing to spend large sums on things such as a lavish new wardrobe for the current social season, made by the most sought-after dressmaker in London, or the extravagant ball she had planned for the end of the coming week.

While Gerard liked money as well as the next fellow and was glad to have an abundance of it, it was not the be all and end all to him, as it seemed to be for so many others of his acquaintance, his mother included.

He had no doubt that if the family should suddenly lose all their wealth, he would make the necessary adjustments in order to survive. While his mother would take to her bed and proclaim that she could not go on.

Barring any such unanticipated catastrophes of utter financial ruin, Gerard and his older brother, Thomas, were expected to take over the family interests one day. Thus, their father had insisted that Gerard's education was arranged in a similar manner to his older brother, with an eye toward that future.

Thomas was currently on the continent, meeting a number of men whom William Hawk had business dealings with.

Gerard had come up to London for his mother's annual ball, but he would be returning to the university shortly afterward to resume his studies. He much preferred life there to the quarterly visits to his parents' townhouse that his mother insisted upon.

Mrs. Phipps drew him from his musings when she spoke again. "But I'm sure you didn't seek me out to discuss the proper treatment of one of the extra servants who has been hired for the ball."

No, he had not. But only because he'd had no knowledge of Fern's existence.

When his mother had stated her intention to ring for a maid

to fetch the housekeeper in order to finalize the menu planned for the ball, Gerard had offered to speak with the housekeeper on his way out of the house before heading to meet with some of his friends at the theater.

However, after learning of the injustice done to Fern by Mrs. Phipps, he desired to conclude this interview with all possible haste and rush out of here, in hopes that he might catch her before she disappeared into the warren of tenements, opium dens, and flash houses that made up the poorer areas of London.

Although he had no notion of where she resided, he could hazard a guess, and she likely lived in a neighborhood that he wouldn't want to walk through alone at night, such as Whitechapel, Old Nichol, or Bethnal Green. Even given Gerard's considerable height and breadth, he would prove no match for a gang of street tough or pickpockets who called London's East End home.

Mrs. Phipps quite possibly knew where Fern was headed, but he didn't put the question to her because he had no wish for the housekeeper to know what he was about. Not that *he* was entirely certain of what he was about, but he preferred to not give rise to speculation.

He felt compelled to go after Fern, to try to somehow make amends for Mrs. Phipps unkind words and callous manner toward her. Fern had a bit of a head start on him as it was, and he hoped she wasn't already so far away as to make it impossible for him to find her tonight.

Anxious to take his leave, he relayed his mother's message. "As to my purpose in coming here, it is to inform you that Mother requests you attend her in the sitting room to go over the selection of foods to be served at the ball."

Giving the housekeeper a curt nod in parting, he turned from her to make his way toward the front door of the grand home.

As he collected his hat and coat before setting out, Gerard refused to consider too closely why the well-being of a poor young woman who was a stranger to him suddenly seemed to matter so much.

CHAPTER 5

Gerard descended the front steps of the townhouse and turned down the street in the direction that would lead to the poorest areas of London.

He didn't want to take the time to have his horse saddled or wait for a carriage to be brought around, fearing that if he didn't set out on foot at once, he'd lose any chance he might have of tracking down Fern before she returned the next day.

He wished to ensure that she would not go hungry this night because of Mrs. Phipps' needlessly harsh actions.

When he reached the larger road a short distance from the townhouse, he looked both ways, searching for a glimpse of Fern.

Was that her bright red hair he could see a few blocks away, moving along at a brisk clip among the heads of other pedestrians? Though he didn't know exactly where she was going, he intended to follow her the whole way there, if he must. Hopefully, it wouldn't come to that, however.

Dodging children playing and street vendors hawking their wares, Gerard endeavored to close the gap between himself and the woman. His longer strides quickly shrank the distance that separated them. As he drew nearer to his quarry, he grew ever more certain that he had guessed her identity correctly.

"Fern!" he called out to her to gain her attention.

Relief filled him as the red head in front of him halted her steps, and he saw that he hadn't made a fool of himself—nor been led off course—by following the wrong woman.

"Please, wait," he added when she turned back toward him to ascertain who had hailed her. "Might I speak with you for a moment?"

Since she didn't immediately deny his request, he increased his pace toward the spot where she waited on the pavement for him.

She was wearing a shabby coat with holes, frayed cuffs, and several buttons missing, which seemed to do little to ward off the chill of approaching nightfall. A patched and worn dress peeked out beneath the hem of the thin, woolen outer garment. Her red hair was pinned in a loose knot at her nape, and several strands had escaped from their confines, catching the last rays of the setting sun. Her blue eyes reminded him of a still lake on a cloudless summer day, when the sky reflected as brilliantly on the surface of the water as though it were a mirror, yet concealing everything that lurked below the surface.

Fern's gaze appeared just as unfathomable as he approached her. She seemed unconcerned that a strange man had stopped her on the street, but there were plenty of other people around, hurrying about their business.

When Gerard reached Fern's side at last, he was slightly out of breath from his own haste. "Please, forgive me for addressing you so familiarly, but I'm afraid I don't know your surname."

"It's Hall. But you may call me Fern." Soft color tinged her cheeks, as she looked up at him with an expectant expression on her face. "And you are?" she prompted when the silence had stretched on for just a touch too long.

"We met just briefly only a short time ago, in the servants quarters at—"

"Yes, I know. I recognize you from before. However, I don't know who you are." Her voice sounded more curious than wary.

He felt embarrassment heating his skin. It seemed that he had forgotten his manners entirely. "Oh, yes, of course. My apologies. I'm Gerard Hawk," he introduced himself.

"Hawk?"

"Yes."

Her eyelashes fluttered down to hide her gaze from his view, and she took a step back from him. It was not the reaction he had expected, but obviously she hadn't realized during their brief encounter in the hallway that he was the second son of the family who employed her on a temporary basis. He could understand how that knowledge might prove a bit intimidating for a young girl in her situation.

He opened his mouth to say something that he hoped would serve to put her at ease, but she spoke before he had the chance.

"Why are you following me? And how do you know my name, Mr. Hawk?"

He felt ridiculous being addressed as Mr. Hawk by this girl who he doubted was more than a handful of years younger than him. "Please, call me Gerard." When she remained silent, ignoring his invitation, he cleared his throat awkwardly. "Yes, well, as to the rest, I must confess to hearing a bit of your conversation with Mrs. Phipps. I questioned her about it, and I must tell you that I was not pleased to learn she had withheld a portion of your wages."

Fern's auburn eyebrows pinched together above the bridge of her nose. "She believed it was warranted given the fact that I broke one of Mrs. Hawk's teacups."

"That's of no true import. It's certainly not sufficient reason for Mrs. Phipps to deny what's owed to you. I'd like to offer my apologies on behalf of our housekeeper. You deserve a fair wage for your work." He slipped his hand into the pocket of his overcoat and extracted a handful of coins. He hadn't known this was what he intended to do until this very moment. "Allow me to pay you the amount of the deficient."

Fern took another step back, putting even more distance between them. "Please put that away, Mr. Hawk. I thank you for your generous offer, but I cannot accept it. It's not your responsibility to provide reparation or apology for another's actions. If you'll excuse me, I must be on my way now."

He reached toward her to stop her from leaving, but he pulled back before he made contact with any part of her person, his hand hovering awkwardly, suspended in the air between them for a moment. "Won't you reconsider?"

She shook her head regretfully, even as her expression firmed with stubborn resolve. "I'm sorry, but no."

Whether she felt regret that she was turning down his offer, or simply regretting her shortage of coins, he could not say. He wondered if it was deep-seated principles—or mere pride —that kept her from accepting. Either way, she did not waver.

He only wanted to ensure her well-being, but he could not compel her to allow him that.

His fingers curled into a fist, his arm dropping to his side.

"Very well, then. In that case, I won't keep you any longer. I shall wish you good day, Fern." Tucking the coins back in his pocket, he executed a shallow bow, then pivoted on his heels to return from whence he'd come.

Even as the distance between them increased, he couldn't deny that he felt drawn to Fern, and his thoughts remained with her as she stood motionless on the street behind him. Yet, he forced himself to keep putting one foot in front of the other, refusing to look back.

If Fern changed her mind, she would surely call out to him before he moved out of earshot.

But no call came.

THIS TIME, FERN WAS THE ONE LEFT TO WATCH, AS GERARD Hawk walked away from her. Not that she had known who he was in that brief moment their gazes had connected before she'd left his parents' townhouse. And to think, she'd imagined he was a mere tradesman, when he was the son of the one of the wealthy merchants in London. What had he been doing in the servants' quarters?

She was mortified to realize that he had overheard Mrs. Phipps taking Fern to task over her clumsiness, though he didn't seem to hold her to blame for the accident. He was nothing like she'd imagined the spoiled young sons of London's moneyed class to be.

Once she lost sight of him among the horses and carriages rumbling past, and the people scurrying to and fro, she shook herself out of her frozen state. Turning back in the direction she'd been heading before he had waylaid her, she hurried toward the Home for Indigent Girls located in the squalor of the East End.

It was a long walk back to the Home, where Matron would be waiting to take the few coins Fern had earned, and more chores were expected of her before she could fall into bed for a few short hours of sleep. Then she would be up once more before the sunrise, to start the seemingly endless cycle all over again.

Fern's stomach growled with hunger, and she needed to make haste if she wanted to arrive before supper was finished. She was lucky if she was given a bit of bread and water at noon while working in the homes of wealthy personages, but many times—today included—she went without until she returned to orphanage at the end of the day.

The Home was far from a haven, however, as little had changed over the past three years since Pearl left.

Fern still didn't know for certain what had become of the little girl. And she had no way to find out. Pearl hadn't returned to the orphanage as had Molly Browne. But whether that was a good thing, or not...? Fern tried very hard not to think about the latter. She prayed every night that wherever Pearl was, she was safe and happy there.

Fern had scarcely stepped through the front door of the Home before Matron was suddenly standing in front of her with her hand outstretched. Fern fished the few coins from her pocket and dropped them into the older woman's open palm.

"What's this?" Matron brought her hand up to her face and squinted down at the pitiful sum of coins she held, as though she was having difficulty seeing. Then she turned her flinty stare to Fern. "Is there a hole in the pocket of that dress?" she demanded.

Fern gripped bunches of the fabric in her fists, her heart began pounding in her chest, as if trying to escape. "No, Matron."

The older woman's dark eyebrows beetled together in a straight line across her forehead. "You worked a full day, yet only came back with a quarter day's wage. Explain to me how that is possible," she ordered, her tone hard.

"I accidentally broke a teacup while I was washing the dishes, and Mrs. Phipps took the cost for its replacement out of my wages."

Matron's eyes narrowed. "Are you telling me lies?"

"No, it's the truth, Matron."

The older woman shook her head in rejection of Fern's words.

"You can ask Mrs. Phipps, if you don't believe me," Fern challenged the older woman.

"Don't think I wouldn't do it. But there's no need to bother her over this matter in order to catch you in a lie. I know exactly who is responsible for the missing money. Did you truly expect to get away with stealing that money and then telling such a ridiculous falsehood to try to cover up your crime?"

Suddenly, Fern questioned the wisdom in turning down Gerard Hawk's offer. But she couldn't have accepted his money, no matter that Matron was angered. Fern would likely be made to suffer the consequences.

She decided against mentioning the conversation with Gerard to Matron now. The older woman would only accuse Fern of compounding her sins by telling more lies to try to get out of trouble.

Matron's dark eyes flashed with fury. "Now where is the money you stole?"

"I don't have it, Matron. I'm telling you the truth, I promise you."

"We shall see about that. After all these years, one might have expected that you would have learned your lesson by now. But it would appear not. So be it. You leave me with no choice but to punish you. Perhaps a few strikes with the cane will compel you to confess."

She reached for the thin, wooden cane, and Fern knew what was coming next. Just as she knew there was no way to avoid it. Not once Matron had made up her mind about the way of things.

Fern knew that no matter what she said in her own defense, Matron wouldn't believe her. The older woman was convinced that she already knew the truth, and nothing Fern could say or do would persuade Matron otherwise.

Sadly, Fern was no stranger to canings. That didn't lessen the sting of the thin length of wood striking her back, however.

❧

EVEN WITH HER THROBBING BACK, SHE WAS EXPECTED TO complete her chores. And once she was able to seek out her bed at last, the pain kept her awake for most of the night, so that by the time morning came, she was tired, achy, and out of sorts. Yet, she had to return to the Hawks' townhouse, where she was immediately put back to work once again by Mrs. Phipps, who proved to be wholly unsympathetic to Fern's plight.

The older woman yelled at Fern, calling her lazy and hurling other insults and invocations when Fern was a bit slower in finishing a task due to the persistent tenderness in her back.

CHAPTER 6

Gerard came upon Fern in the front parlor, dusting his mother's prized collection of jade figurines. The older woman was determined that every inch of the townhouse would be spotless by the time the first guests arrived on the day of the ball, and Gerard couldn't seem to find a space in the house that wasn't occupied by one industrious servant or another. And yet, still his mother fretted that everything wouldn't be done in time.

He had just been contemplating going for a horseback ride to escape the chaos when he'd caught sight of familiar red hair trying to escape its pins, and he immediately changed course without conscious volition. One moment, he had been intending to head to the stables, and the next, he was walking through the doorway into the parlor. Now, he found he had no desire to follow through on his original intent.

"Good afternoon, Fern," he greeted her.

She started in surprise at the sound of his voice, and she winced as her feather duster sent a green piece of jade sailing off the shelf to land with a loud thud against the hard floor. "Oh, no!" she cried.

"Please accept my apologies. It was entirely my fault. I didn't mean to startle you."

She didn't acknowledge his words, as she wrung her hands and bit down on her bottom lip. "I hope it's not damaged. I can't afford to lose any more of my wages." That last part had been spoken under her breath.

Gerard didn't think she'd meant for him to hear it, so he refrained from remarking that his offer from the day before remained open. Even if he had to cover the cost of this mishap as well—which truly had been his fault, not hers. So, if anyone was made to pay to replace the piece of jade, he would insist that it be him.

Although Fern was plainly worried that the jade figurine might have come to some harm, it seemed that reluctance won out over moving across the room to check the carved stone's condition.

He bent down to pick it up, and ran his hand over the familiar chipped edge, then placed the figurine back on the shelf. "There now, no harm done," he assured her with a smile, hoping to ease her anxiety.

"I don't know anything about fancy items like this, but I'm sure it would have cost much more to replace this than a single china teacup." She leaned slightly forward for a closer inspection, and then gasped.

His smile slipped from his face as all the color seemed to leach out of her fair complexion, and he reached out to steady her by taking hold of her hand.

Fern looked as though she might be sick, her blue eyes appearing larger against her ashen skin. "There's a chip out of the corner. I'll have to work here for free for a more than year, as least, in order to repay this kind of debt."

"That won't be necessary. My brother is the person responsible for that chip, not you."

It took a moment before his words seemed to register amid her troubled thoughts. When they finally did, she turned her gaze to Gerard with a hopeful expression. "Your brother damaged the figurine?"

"Yes, he thought it would be grand fun to have his tin soldiers attack the ranks of jade invaders. He had no appreciation for the fine craftsmanship of the pieces. Of course, he was only five years old at the time. He's developed a more refined taste since then," he said to lighten the mood.

Yet, a line of worry appeared between Fern's eyebrows. "Your brother truly damaged the jade figurine? You're not merely saying that so that I don't get in trouble again with Mrs.

Phipps?" She pulled her hand back from him, and he was forced to let her go.

He had told her the absolute truth—but even if it had been nothing more than a fabricated tale, he wouldn't have admitted it to Fern. "You have nothing to fear from Mrs. Phipps in that regard, I assure you."

She didn't look as though she quite believed him, but she didn't argue against his claim. "I need to return to work, before she comes in here and finds me doing nothing."

Gerard took a step back from her, not wanting the house-keeper to reprimand Fern for neglecting her duties. He didn't wish to cause her any further distress.

But as he prepared to take his leave of her, he noticed that she seemed to be holding herself rather stiffly. And when she moved to resume her dusting, a wince of pain tightened her features for a brief moment.

He tilted his head to the side, considering her through narrowed eyes. "What's wrong?"

She turned to face him once more, one eyebrow arching in inquiry. "What do you mean?"

"Your movements appear to pain you today. Yet, I didn't notice anything amiss yesterday evening."

Her cheeks reddened at his words. "It's nothing."

He took a step closer to her, and she responded by taking an equal step back from him. The heel of her shoe caught on the edge of an Aubusson carpet, causing her to trip backwards.

Gerard quickly reached for her to keep her from falling, one arm wrapping around her waist, and his hand landing against her back.

She instantly flinched away from his touch and shoved out of his hold.

"I'm sorry," he apologized. "Are you all right?"

"I'm fine."

He hadn't expected any other answer from her, as he'd already surmised during their brief acquaintance that she seemed unwilling to acknowledge any sort of weakness. But he knew she wasn't being completely honest with him.

"That wasn't nothing. Is it your back that's injured? Or somewhere else?"

"Yes."

He shook his head in confusion. "Yes, what?"

She pressed her lips together, and for a handful of seconds, he thought she wouldn't respond.

"It hurt when you touched my back."

"Why?"

She hesitated for another long moment. But once she finally

got started, it was easier to coax her to continue. She poured
out the whole sorry tale.

When she fell silent again, he felt equal parts sorrow for what
Fern had suffered and rage at the woman who had inflicted
such suffering on her. And for what? Merely because the
matron of the orphanage refused to believe that Fern was
telling her the truth.

"Perhaps the cook might have a salve that will help soothe the
pain," he suggested.

"Thank you for your concern. But I'm all right. Truly. I'm used
to working with this sort of injury."

Gerard was appalled by her words, spoken in such a calm
manner, making it clear that this was nothing out of the ordi-
nary for Fern.

He couldn't let her go back to that place. But what was the
alternative?

Leaving Fern alone in the front parlor, he went in search of
his mother, to put forth the idea that had just come to him.
He found his mother in her sitting room, enjoying a cup of tea
and a plate of scones.

After he greeted her, and she'd offered him refreshments, he
jumped right into the purpose of his visit to her. After making
mention of the beating Fern had endured the night before, he
suggested that his mother hire Fern on a more permanent

basis by making her a part of the regular staff, so that she would not have to return to the orphanage.

He was disappointed—but not surprised—when the older woman waved away his concerns regarding Fern.

"I cannot be bothered with the troubles of one of the temporary maids right now, Gerard," she stated, her expression remaining unchanged from what it had been prior to his revelation of Fern's circumstances. "I have too much to do to prepare for the Ball."

Though he was under no allusions about that which his mother valued most—herself—he had hoped to appeal to her better nature. A thing which he'd often found himself questioning whether it existed at all.

His mother's selfish nature left little room for consideration of others, her own wants and desires winning out above all else. Although she showed a bit of warmth and affection toward Gerard and his older brother, Thomas, they seemed to be the only ones for whom she held a measure of regard. Even her husband, Gerard's father, was viewed with an eye toward what his wealth could provide her, rather than with any sort of fond sentiment for the man himself.

Pushing aside that oft-pondered thought, Gerard turned his mind back to the matter at hand.

Having failed to gain the outcome he desired by other means, he tried a different tact. "Perhaps Fern can be of some additional assistance with preparations for the ball. If she did not have to travel to and from the orphanage each day, she might have time to complete another task or two."

He didn't wish for Fern to have to work anymore than she already must, but he'd had to say something that would persuade his mother—and that meant pointing out how Fern's presence could be of benefit to the older woman.

"Hum," she responded, considering his words. "Perhaps you're correct. I suppose I could instruct Mrs. Phipps to set up a pallet for the girl in the kitchen. Mrs. Phipps can see to the details, including sending a note around to the orphanage to inform the matron not to expect the girl back for the remainder of the week. She can stay here until the day after the ball."

Gerard had hoped for more than that—but it was better than nothing. And it would give him a few days in which to try to convince his mother to reconsider sending Fern back to that horrible place.

LATER THAT DAY, FERN SOUGHT OUT THE HOUSEKEEPER TO collect her wages before returning to the Home for Indigent Girls, where she knew she would be expected to do yet more chores despite the throbbing ache in her back.

"You won't be leaving just yet," Mrs. Phipps informed her.

"What?" Shock and worry filled Fern.

Had she not completed one of her tasks up to the older woman's exacting standards? Or did Mrs. Phipps have a list of other things that she required Fern to do before she could depart? Her shoulders slumped at the thought.

"There's much more to be done in preparation for the ball," the housekeeper imparted. "Mrs. Hawk has determined that you shall remain here for another two or three days, until after the ball, in order to ensure that nothing will be left undone."

"Oh, but—"

Had Matron agreed to this new arrangement? Perhaps 'agreed' wasn't the correct word, but if Mrs. Hawk had decided it, the other woman wouldn't dare to gainsay her.

"There are a few more tasks I'll need you to complete tonight, before you join the other servants for supper," the house-keeper continued, seeming unaware of Fern's confused reaction to the sudden and unexpected change in the terms of her employment status. "Then, I'll show you where you'll be sleeping. I'll hold your wages until the day your temporary employment here ends, instead of paying you daily."

Fern didn't argue with the housekeeper's directions. She merely nodded in acknowledgement and followed behind her, as the older woman went over Fern's additional assigned tasks.

WHEN FERN SETTLED INTO HER BED IN THE KITCHEN LATER that night, her belly was full. The pallet was a bit uncomfortable, but no more so than the lumpy mattress at the orphanage. Here, there were no little feet kicking her under the blanket. And the heat from the cook stove kept her warm. All in all, it was an improvement over the nights she was used to enduring at the Home.

Yet, she couldn't sleep. Though tiredness dragged at her body, thoughts of her uncertain future filled her head, keeping her awake.

She would have to leave the Home in a little more than a year and search to find some sort of position in order to support herself. She would most likely look for permanent work as a maid, even though she hated having to take orders from anyone like Mrs. Phipps, who was a harsh taskmaster. What if all housekeepers were of a similar disposition?

But at least she'd no longer have to hand over her wages to Matron. Oh, what joy to be able to spend her small earnings however she liked. Although most of it would probably go to food and other necessities, she might be able to purchase a treat or two for herself as well.

Despite those hopeful thoughts, she feared that it would prove to be a much harder existence than she might imagine.

If she couldn't find work, she would not eat—and she wouldn't be able to sustain herself for long without food.

It was difficult to imagine that her situation could get any worse, but she knew it was all too possible.

She got up to fetch herself a drink of water, then decided to go out into the back garden for a bit, in hopes that the night air might serve to still her mind.

The back door opened soundlessly beneath her hand, and she stepped outside.

She wandered along the gravel paths, past flowerbeds and a fountain with fanciful mermaids. Rounding a boxwood hedge with leaves that appeared almost black in the darkness, she stopped suddenly as she saw the large, dark figure of a man posed motionless beneath the branches of a tree.

She froze in indecision. She wasn't ready to return to her bed in the kitchen just yet, but neither did she wish to place herself in a dangerous situation. Glancing back at the darkened windows of the house behind her, she knew that the rest of the household was asleep, unable to come to her aid should there be a need.

She started to turn away from the shadowy figure.

"Fern."

The sound of her name drifted to her on the still night air.

She recognized Gerard's voice instantly, and the apprehension she had been feeling a moment ago drained out of her.

As she drew closer, she could see that he was sitting on a stone bench. The moon came out from behind a cloud just then, and she could see his expression clearly.

He didn't appear surprised to find her walking the gardens at midnight. Had he known that his mother would insist on Fern staying at the townhouse for a few days? Or did he have something to do with his mother's sudden decision to keep her here until after the ball? Fern wondered, remembering his reaction to learning of her confrontation with Matron, and the subsequent punishment for her supposed lies.

Gerard hadn't said anything at the time, but Fern had sensed the outrage and horror he'd felt.

Now that the thought has occurred to her, she suspected that he had played a part in this day's startling turn of events. But she didn't voice the question because she didn't wish to risk shattering the moment by reminding him of her grim circumstances.

"Join me," he invited.

"I should return inside," she replied, but she didn't move to do so.

"Stay and talk with me for a while," he requested.

"All right," she agreed after a small hesitation.

She *should* go back inside and try to fall asleep. Even if she couldn't sleep, she still shouldn't stay out here alone in the dark with Gerard. Not because she feared coming to any harm from him—at least not physically. But because her feelings for him were growing stronger than was safe.

She admired his compassion and kindness. Whenever their gazes met, he acknowledged her, instead of looking through her and acting as though she didn't exist, or that she was beneath his notice. This was unlike most of the wealthy inhabitants of the grand houses where she had worked as a maid, cleaning and performing kitchen duties.

If she was not careful, she could easily fall in love with Gerard. But nothing could ever come of it. He was much too far above her in station, so far above her reach that he might as well be living among the stars. She could more easily imagine herself touching those stars than sharing a life with Gerard.

Oh, but what was she thinking? Her mind was running away into places where it had no business. His parents would never allow him to marry a penniless, orphaned girl who worked as a maid in their home.

Besides, she didn't really know Gerard. At least not that well...

But it seemed like she did. Deep in her heart, it seemed like she did. She shuddered. She needed to remember who she was. Spending more time in his company would start her foolish heart wishing for impossible things.

Gerard shifted slightly to make room for her on the stone bench.

She ignored the voice of caution in her head.

CHAPTER 7

Fern moved forward and sat down next to Gerard on the hard, cold stone bench. "What are you doing out here?" she asked him before he had the chance to put the question to her.

"Just thinking about things."

That piqued her curiosity. "Such as?"

He didn't seem to take offense at her unmannerly inquiry. "Such as the fact that I'll be returning to school shortly after the ball."

Her heart sank slightly at his words, but she ignored it. "What's it like, learning about so many different things?" she asked.

The girls at the orphanage were given a basic education, but there were a great number of topics for further study of which Fern had no understanding.

"The university offers instruction in all manner of subjects. Ancient history and languages are of particular interest to me. However, my father insists on courses teaching finances and business."

As he continued relaying details of his school experiences, Fern wished that she too could attend university. But she didn't have the kind of money necessary for such an endeavor —or any money at all, in truth. Nor did she likely have the brains for it.

But she refused to allow such grim thoughts to intrude on this shared moment with Gerard. She loved listening to his deep voice, telling amusing tales that elicited laughter, which was in sadly short supply in Fern's life.

At last, he fell silent, and they sat together without speaking for several seconds, until he asked, "Does your back still pain you?"

"Not as much as earlier." Though it would be several days before the tenderness was gone completely, as Fern knew from personal experience.

"From what you've told me so far, it sounds like a grim existence living in The Home for Indigent Girls, with a heartless woman running things."

Fern didn't want to talk anymore about Matron or her life at the orphanage. Instead she told him stories about the small joys she'd found with Pearl. All the while, hiding her doubts about the little girl's current circumstances and well-being.

"You were close to her?" Gerard asked.

"Yes. She was only at the Home for a few months. But I miss her still, even though it's been three years since she left the orphanage. She's seven years younger than me, so she would be about nine or ten years old now." The same age Fern had been when her mother abandoned her in the market that long-ago day and Matron had found her and taken her to live at the orphanage.

Fern shook herself from those thoughts and focused back on the present, her gaze fixed on Gerard.

❧

AFTER THAT NIGHT IN THE GARDEN, THE NEXT SEVERAL nights followed a similar pattern. Each time Fern left her bed in hopes of encountering him again, she found him sitting on the stone bench. But she would never admit aloud that her true purpose in going out to the gardens at night was to see him.

Fern was kept busy during the day, helping with preparations for the ball, and she only caught brief glimpses of Gerard during the hours of daylight. But at night, when she ventured out to the garden, he was always there, waiting for her.

He seemed to enjoy her company as much as she enjoyed his, and they talked about all manner of things. But she knew that no matter how friendly and open Gerard was with her, there could never be anything more between them than those precious, stolen moments together. And those too might be snatched away from her if anyone learned of their meetings and told his parents. Mr. and Mrs. Hawk would no doubt insist that he cease the unseemly association with her at once.

Even if it remained a secret, Fern would be returning to the orphanage the day after the ball anyway. So, while she was grateful to share even a single happy moment with Gerard, she knew it couldn't last.

But it ended sooner than she'd anticipated.

During the evening of the ball, Fern was pressed into service, carrying trays with cups of punch and champagne, and replenishing the refreshments table. Or she was sent on errands by some of the guests, to repair a damaged hem or fetch a vial of smelling salts.

It was near dawn by the time the guests began to depart, and the servants were required to clean up the mess left behind before they could seek their beds. Fern joined several other maids and set to work sweeping up crumpled napkins and other debris scattered on the floor in the ballroom, while the last few guests waited in the front foyer as the butler retrieved gloves, cloaks, and hats.

Two loud handclaps startled Fern, and she turned to see Mrs. Phipps standing at the open double doors. The older woman stepped forward now that she'd gained their attention.

"Every one of you must return to the servants' quarters at once, but you are not permitted to go into your rooms." She turned without another word and left the room.

Fern looked at the other maids in confusion, but none of the other girls seemed to have any more of an idea what was going on than Fern did.

"We'd best hurry," a maid with dark hair said. "Mrs. Phipps has no patience for those that dawdle."

Fern made her way to the servants' quarters with the others to find that the entire household staff had been gathered.

"Something must have gone missing," one of the kitchen maids speculated.

Suddenly Mrs. Phipps and the butler, Mr. Lands, appeared before the assembled servants. The older man stood back while the housekeeper addressed the group.

"A fur-lined cape disappeared from the cloakroom sometime during the Ball. Much unpleasantness can be avoided if the guilty party steps forward now and confesses.

Fern glanced around at the others standing nearest her and noticed that they were all doing the same. No one spoke up.

"Very well, then." The housekeeper unhooked her ring of keys from her belt. "Mr. Lands and I will conduct a search of the servants' quarters. No one is to leave here until the search is completed."

As soon as the two had departed in the company of several footmen, a buzz of whispering began among the remaining servants.

A short time later Mrs. Phipps and Mr. Lands returned, and the servants fell silent once more.

The housekeeper's gaze scanned the room. "There she is," she pronounced, pointing in Fern's direction. "Lock her in the small storage room off the kitchen while the police are sent for."

Fern turned to glance behind her to see who Mrs. Phipps was speaking of, but no one appeared overly fearful at being caught.

Fern was taken by surprise when two burly footmen seized her and began to pull her toward the kitchen. "What's going on?"

"The cape was found hidden under your pallet," Mrs. Phipps informed her.

"What?" She gasped in shock, then started struggling against the footmen's hold. "But I didn't take it."

The older woman didn't believe her, however. "You can tell that to the police. I don't know if you thought to steal the cape to make up for the wages you lost due to your carelessness in breaking a teacup, but I assure you that the magistrate with not look kindly on that sort of justification for your actions."

"I didn't take the cape," Fern repeated.

But no one was listening to her, and she shortly found herself locked in a small, dark room not much bigger than the broom closet at the Home for Indigent Girls. There was no chair to sit on, so she sank down to the floor, pulled her knees up to her chest and wrapped her arms around them, then laid her head against her up-drawn legs.

She was believed guilty, and she doubted the police would look too hard for evidence that might prove her innocence. For most of her life, she had been beneath others' notice. To put it bluntly, she was simply not worth their bother. She did not delude herself about most people's opinions of abandoned and orphaned girls.

No one would care what happened to her now.

GERARD WAS SHOCKED WHEN HE LEARNED THAT FERN HAD

been locked up under suspicion that she had stolen the cape. Not for one second did he believe that she was guilty of the crime. Over the course of the past several days, he'd come to know her well enough to correctly judge her character. If she would not even accept his offer of a few coins freely given, she'd never think of stealing such a costly item as a fur-lined cape from one of the guests in attendance at the Hawks' Ball.

He went to speak to his father at once, to straighten out the matter.

"I don't believe that Fern Hall is responsible for the theft," Gerard explained as he stood in his father's study and faced the older man seated behind a wide mahogany desk.

William Hawk's dark eyebrows knit together above the bridge of his slightly overlarge nose. "But the cape was found concealed under her sleeping pallet in the kitchen."

"That doesn't prove that she's the one who put it there. Dozens of servants have access to the kitchen, and any one of them could have done it.

"That's a matter for the police to decide," the older man dismissed Gerard's concerns, turning his attention back to the documents spread out before him.

Gerard pivoted on his heels and quit the room. But though he had not stayed to continue pleading Fern's case to his father, he did not intend to stand aside and do nothing in the face of this injustice.

He took the back servants' stairs to reach the storage room off the kitchen.

The key scraped in the lock, and he pushed open the door to find Fern huddled in a dejected heap on the hard, wooden floor.

She raised her head, her blue eyes appearing darker in the dim interior of the tiny room. "Gerard?"

"We don't have much time." He stepped back from the doorway. "Go now."

"What?" she asked, remaining motionless on the floor.

"You must leave here before the police arrive."

She pushed to her feet. "You're releasing me?"

"Yes. Because I know you are innocent of the charge."

Hope lit her expression. "You do?"

He nodded once in response. "But the police might not see things that way." Gerard had no proof of his conviction, and the authorities might view the location where the cape was found as irrefutable evidence of Fern's guilt. "I won't allow you to be wrongfully punished for another crime you didn't commit."

Tears filled her eyes, but she blinked. Her lashes kept them from falling. "Thank you, Gerard."

"Thanks are not necessary. It's the right thing to do."

She surprised him by wrapping her arms around him in a tight hug. "I've never known a better man than you."

He returned her embrace for a handful of seconds, but all too soon he had to force himself to relinquish his hold. "Go."

He didn't have to tell her again, as she took to her heels. He watched her retreating figure until she had vanished through the door leading out to the gardens. He waited another three-quarters of an hour by the closed door of the small room to ensure that no one discovered Fern's disappearance too soon.

When the police arrived, Gerard confessed to his actions, so that none of the servants would be blamed for helping Fern to escape.

"The cape has been returned to the guest," Gerard said in a bid to convince the authorities not to chase after Fern.

One of the constables threw up his hands in frustration at having made a wasted trip to the Hawks' house, but no more was said about the incident before the uniformed men departed.

❦

THE FOLLOWING DAY, GERARD TRAVELED TO THE HOME for Indigent Girls to check on Fern only to discover that she hadn't returned there after leaving his family's house—a fact over which the matron did not hesitate to make her displeasure known.

Gerard was glad that Fern had not come back to this grim and horrible place. Yet, he feared that wherever she was now, it might prove to be far worse.

Over the course of the next several days before he was forced to return to school, Gerard spent countless hours going to the kinds of places where no sane person would dare set foot unless they had no choice. And Gerard did not feel he had a choice in his search for Fern. But it was as though she'd vanished into thin air—or rather into the maze of refuse-littered streets that made up the most dangerous and foul areas of London.

Though it pained him, he had to accept that he would probably never see her again. He rubbed at the ache in his chest that felt almost physical, throbbing in the region directly over his heart.

PART III

CHAPTER 8

A Year and a Half Later...

AN ENVELOPE DROPPED ONTO THE WORK DESK IN FRONT OF Fern, amid the ribbons and silk flowers she was attaching to the brim of a turquoise ladies' hat.

"What's this?" she asked, looking up at the owner of the milliner's shop where Fern had found work a year before.

"Don't know," Mrs. Wellburn grunted before pushing through the curtain to return to the front of the shop.

Fern reached to pick up the envelope and turned it over, noticing that it was addressed to her. How curious. She broke open the seal and a handful of coins plunked onto the wooden table. There could be no mistaking that the money was intended for her, but who could be sending it? She struggled to read the enclosed note, finally figuring out that it merely gave the direction of a solicitor, Silas Finnegan. She didn't recognize the name, and she didn't know the man.

"Where did that money come from?" Mrs. Wellburn demanded, having appeared suddenly behind Fern without her awareness.

"It was in the envelope," she replied, tucking the coins and the solicitor's card into her apron pocket, then returning to her work before the older woman reprimanded her for idleness.

"You aren't planning on leaving me in the lurch now that you're a little flush in the pockets, are you?"

"Of course not, Mrs. Wellburn."

"Good."

The bell on the millinery's front door rang just then, and the older woman returned to the front of the shop to attend to the customer.

Fern startled at the sound of a familiar voice conversing with the Mrs. Wellburn, and she just barely avoided pricking her finger with the needle she was using to affix a bit of peach ribbon to the hat.

Setting her work aside once more, she crept toward the

curtain separating the workroom from the front of the shop and lifted a corner of the fabric to peer through the doorway.

She spotted Mrs. Hawk standing a short distance away. She glanced around the shop, hoping to see Gerard, but was not surprised to discover that he had not accompanied his mother to the millinery. She could not deny her disappointment, as she let the curtain fall back into place.

Later that night, she could not ignore the impulse to walk pass the Hawks' home before returning to the tenement apartment where she lived with several others. Gaslights lit her way along the cobblestone roads.

For a moment, she thought someone was following her, as footfalls sounded behind her, but when she turned down the street where the Hawks' house was located and then looked behind her, there was no one there.

Standing in front of the wrought-iron railing between the Hawks' brick townhouse and the street, she looked up at the lighted windows concealed behind heavy drapes. Did Gerard still reside with his parents?

Something compelled her to walk around the block and down the alley to the mews at the back of the house, in hopes that she might find Gerard sitting on the same stone bench as she had for those few wonderful nights so long ago. Though it was probably a foolish wish, and she doubted he would truly be there.

She gasped in shock when she spotted a dark figure, not on the stone bench but under the tree. Was it Gerard? She moved closer, trying to get a glimpse of the man's face in the weak light from the quarter moon.

As she stepped forward, her shoe knocked into something that caused a horrible racket and a dog set to barking nearby.

Fern's heart started pounding as she spun around and dashed off back down the alley.

"Who's there?" she heard Gerard's familiar voice call out behind her.

But she didn't dare halt her flight. She ran all the way home, and by the time she reached the tenement, she was completely out of breath from her misadventure.

However, it seemed that nothing could prevent her from returning to the Hawks' townhouse the next night—and every night after. Until she finally caught sight of Gerard sitting on the stone bench in the garden again.

This time, she set her feet much more carefully, as she edged closer.

۞

GERARD HEARD SOFT FOOTFALLS BEHIND HIM, AND HE turned to see who was trying to sneak up on him in the dead of night.

Even in the dim glow of the moonlight, he could see the red color of her hair.

"Fern," he breathed in wonder, instantly recognizing the young woman standing frozen a short distance from him.

"You remember who I am?" Uncertainly tinged her voice.

"Of course." He would never forget her.

He'd thought of her often over the past year and half. He'd wondered if she was all right.

Pushing up from the stone bench, he approached her. "I searched for you," he revealed. "For days afterward, I tried to find you—but couldn't. Where did you go?"

"Back where I belonged."

He shook his head at her words. "I don't understand. You didn't return to the orphanage. I searched for you there."

"No, I feared that would be the first place the police would look for me."

"After that first week, they weren't looking for you." If they had ever looked for her at all.

"What do you mean?"

"The thefts continued after you left, so it was clear to everyone—even Mrs. Phipps—that you weren't responsible for them. It was a short leap from there to realize that you hadn't stolen the cape that night, either."

"Oh." Her expression showed nothing more than mild curiously.

She didn't seem to bear any ill will toward the one to blame for her misfortune, and he felt awed by her generous spirit and forbearance.

It had been discovered that one of the other maids had been behind the theft of the cape, and had tucked it under Fern's sleeping pallet because it had been a convenient hiding place when someone had come upon her suddenly as she was trying to sneak out the back door. But by the time that truth had been revealed, Fern had already vanished without a trace.

"What did you mean when you said that you'd gone back where you belonged?" he questioned, still puzzled by her earlier words.

"I meant that I don't belong here."

"Here in the garden?"

"In this garden with you, in your family's townhouse, in this area of London filled with affluence and wealth. I mean all of that, Gerard. You're always been kind to me, but I don't belong in your world. All I can hope for is to visit it for a time."

"Fern..." His voice was soft.

"I'm not like you. Or your parents. Or your neighbors." She waved her hand at the row of townhouses bracketing his family's home. "When I left here that night, I owned nothing but the clothes on my back. And to be entirely truthful, I didn't really even own that, since the orphanage had provided the clothing to me, as it does to all the other girls. I was forced to beg on the streets in order to sustain myself, and there were many days when I went hungry.

"I live in a tiny tenement apartment with five other girls, most of whom are pickpockets. Though I would never dare to steal anything after narrowly avoiding arrest that night, I don't condemn them for their unlawful actions. Each of us does what we must to survive. Without any references, I couldn't find a position as a maid. I consider it a stroke of good fortunate that I was able to find work at a ladies hat shop. The wage is small, but it's enough to pay my portion of the rent and buy a bit of food. I'm more fortunate than many."

And much less fortunate than some, he couldn't help but think. He admired her strong will and courage, that she had survived the near-ruin which had befallen her—and could somehow still be grateful to have so little, rather than be resentful for all she did not have.

He wished to give her so much more than what she had come to expect in life, but he knew she wouldn't accept it. At least not material possessions or gifts of a monetary nature. She had never turned down the offer of his friendship.

But he wanted to provide her with more—a lifetime of shared

laughter and smiles, free from financial worries. However, he feared she would never truly believe that their differences didn't matter to him. That she had his affection, and he felt more for her than mere kindness.

He sought to convince her, no matter that he feared it would prove futile.

"Wealth does not equal worth, Fern. And you're worth more than many who possess an overabundance of riches. There will always be those with more money, but that doesn't make them better than you."

"You are the only one of your elevated station who thinks so. I'm of the servant class, and you are at the highest level of the merchant class. It's a gap much too great to bridge."

"I don't—"

"I must go."

And before he could say another word, she'd slipped away in the darkness.

CHAPTER 9

After Fern's last conversation with Gerard, she'd stopping going by the Hawks' townhouse at night. She didn't wish to continue torturing herself with what could never be hers.

She received a few more envelopes with money in them over the course of the next few weeks, but then they suddenly stopped arriving.

She didn't think anything of it, other than that her mysterious benefactor had decided to cease his donations. Of course, she suspected that perhaps Gerard was behind them, but she didn't have any proof. It didn't matter anymore, anyway, after they stopped coming.

But then, while she was looking for a misplaced length of sea-green ribbon, she discovered a handful of opened envelopes with the solicitor's card tucked inside. Only there was no money. She realized that Mrs. Wellburn must be responsible for the missing coins.

She went to confront the older woman. Shockingly, the older woman showed no signs of remorse over her dishonest actions. And what's more, she informed Fern that her two nieces would begin working at the shop, and Fern wouldn't be needed any longer.

Fern was out of a job.

She felt numb as she headed toward the tenement apartment. It was no sort of a home, really, but she still felt a sense of dread that she might soon lose even that much. What was she to do now?

When she reached the tenement, one of the other girls informed her that a man had been there looking for her.

"What did he want?" she questioned, fearing who it might be, remembering the night long ago when she had the eerie feeling that she was being following.

"He didn't say."

Or was it the police? Were they after her despite what Gerard had told her? But there was no reason for the police to be after her, was there? She'd been cleared of the crime from which she had run more than a year ago. And if Matron hadn't sent someone to come after her before now, it made no sense for her to start now.

The next evening, there was a knock at the door, and Fern opened it to reveal a white-haired man with a handlebar mustache.

He doffed his hat to her. "Are you Miss Fern Hall?"

"Yes," she replied cautiously.

"It's a pleasure to meet you, Miss Hall. I'm Silas Finnegan."

She immediately recognized his name from the envelopes that had been delivered the Mrs. Wellburn's shop. "What can I do for you, sir?"

"I'm the solicitor for Mr. Worthing, the father of Pearl Worthing."

"I'm afraid I don't know any Worthings, Mr. Finnegan."

"You don't remember Pearl from the Home for Indigent Girls?"

Fern's lips parted and tears filled her eyes. "Pearl?" she uttered, wondering if she'd heard correctly.

The man smiled, and his moustache twitched. "Yes, Miss Hall. The very same."

Fern clasped her hands to her chest. "Of course I remember Pearl. Mr. Worthing is her father, you said?"

"Yes. It seems that young Pearl has talked of you since she left the orphanage. Mr. Worthing instructed me to locate you and ascertain your situation."

"After all this time?"

"It took us a while to find you, Miss."

"So, the money was from you?"

"Indirectly, yes. I only made sure it was delivered to you. The funds actually came from Mr. Worthing."

This caused a whole host of questions to fill her head, but then another thought occurred to her. "Have you been following me?"

"Yes, to that as well, but only to determine the best way to approach you. Would you like to visit with the Worthings? Pearl is anxious to know if you are well."

Fern wanted to go immediately to see Pearl, but it was late in the day. "I would like nothing more. Nothing."

"I shall inform the Worthings of your agreement to visit them. Would tomorrow be suitable? I shall come for you."

Fern nodded in response, her mind whirling. As soon as the solicitor left, she burst into tears.

THE FOLLOWING DAY FOUND FERN STANDING ON THE Worthings' doorstep. It was a stately townhouse in a respectable neighborhood. Was this truly where Pearl had been living all this time? Had Fern's prayers been answered so beautifully?

The door opened and a blond girl of about eleven rushed out to wrap Fern in a tight hug. "You came!"

When she stepped back, Fern gazed at her precious Pearl. "I can't believe how grown up you look," she marveled.

No longer did Pearl look years younger than her age. Her cheeks were round and rosy, glowing with good health.

Fern noticed an older woman standing behind Pearl.

"Won't you come in, Miss Hall?" the woman invited.

"Thank you, Mrs. Worthing," Fern replied, guessing the woman's identity. "Please, call me Fern."

A short time later, Fern was sitting with Pearl and Mrs. Worthing in the parlor. For the most part, the older woman focused on her embroidery, leaving the two girls to get reacquainted.

"I missed you so much," Pearl remarked.

"I missed you, too. You can't imagine how much."

Pearl leaned against Fern's side. "I have Mama and Papa. But you had no one."

"That's not true. I did have someone," Fern replied, thinking of Gerard.

Pearl's eyebrows scrunched up. "What happened? Did he move away?"

Fern wondered how Pearl had guessed it was a man, but it was of no matter. "Nothing happened. I just haven't seen him in a while."

"Does he live far from you?"

"Yes." Fern didn't bother to explain that she was speaking of more than just a physical distance. Realizing that she was dwelling overmuch on Gerard, she pushed thoughts of him from her mind and focused solely on Pearl. "You look so happy."

"It's just as you told me, Fern. Mama and Papa treat me as though I'm their real daughter."

"You are our real daughter," the older woman interjected from her place on the settee.

Pearl rolled her eyes. "You know what I mean, Mama."

Mrs. Worthing gave Pearl an indulgent smile, then returned to her embroidery.

A half hour full of happy chatter later, Fern regretted that she have to leave.

"I should be getting back home," she said, though what she really meant was that she needed to begin searching for work. She didn't voice that aloud, however.

Mrs. Worthing raised her gaze from her embroidery. "Might you stay a bit longer, Fern? Mr. Worthing would like to speak to you when he returns home from his office."

Fern opened her mouth to decline.

"Yes, please stay," Pearl exclaimed, then turned to her mother. "Fern can stay for supper, can't she?"

"Of course, she can."

Pearl turned a happy smile to Fern, and Fern's heart felt lighter than she could ever remember.

"I would like that," she agreed.

❦

"You offer is generous beyond imagining, but I can't accept it," Fern said to Mr. Worthing later that day.

"Nonsense. I insist. Use the money to start a business."

She shook her head. "I couldn't—"

"I'm an investor, my dear. If you are unable to accept the money as a gift, look on this as an investment,."

"But I don't know anything about running a business," she protested.

He waved her concern aside. "I'll hire a bookkeeper to assist you."

One by one, he had dispatched all of her objections, and Fern finally realized that he wouldn't allow her to turn down his offer to settle an amount on her. He was highly concerned that his beloved daughter never again need worry about Fern's situation. Plus, he was grateful to her for her care of Pearl.

Fern hated to think that Pearl had fretted about her all this time. She certainly didn't want to mar the younger girl's happiness now. Given that, there was only one thing Fern could say.

"How can I ever thank you?"

"It is Mrs. Worthing and I who need to thank you for keeping Pearl safe for us until she was able to come and live with us. So, you'll take the money I'm offering you?"

"Yes."

He nodded his satisfaction. "Well, then, perhaps you can tell me what sort of investment I'm making," he said with a twinkle in his eye. "Mind you, I'm merely curious, is all. There are no stipulations attached."

Fern bit down on her bottom lip. "I don't know. I don't have any experience in anything but hat-making."

"A millinery shop is an excellent idea," he proclaimed, as though Fern had put forth that suggestion, rather than lamenting her lack of skills.

Now that the thought was in her head, she realized that she liked the sound of it. "Fern's Millinery" had a nice ring to it.

As Fern prepared to depart the Worthing townhouse a short time later, Pearl latched onto her as though unable to bear being separated again.

Fern hugged the younger girl close for a moment. "I'll come back to see you again soon," she promised before bidding farewell to Mr. and Mrs. Worthing.

Having found Pearl again at last, Fern wanted to share the happy news with someone. She had been pining for the little girl for years. And now, the only person she could think to share this news with was Gerard. But she forced herself to give up that notion. She was being foolish and letting her heart get away from her.

※

OVER THE NEXT TWO MONTHS, FERN ACCEPTED MR. Worthing's further help in establishing her business. She was ignorant of so much, and he was so patient in teaching her. And the delightful bonus for Fern was being able to see Pearl frequently.

Fern's Millinery opened a month later, amid much fanfare. The initial fervor soon died down, but the shop continued to do a steady business that provided Fern with a comfortable income. Many wealthy women came into the shop to order hats. Fern hired a bookkeeper who handled the business aspects of running the millinery. Fern was only too aware of her limitations in that area. Instead, she focused on creating unique and special hats for her customers.

Two months after her shop opened, the bell over the front door jingled as yet another woman entered the shop. Fern turned to her with a smile on her face, but her expression froze when she recognized Mrs. Hawk.

"May I help you?" she asked, her voice sounding stilted to her own ears.

"Yes, I'd like to order a hat." No recognition showed in the older woman's eyes, and Fern began to relax somewhat.

"Please, come this way, and we can discuss the design," she invited.

Throughout their conversation, Fern had a hard time focusing on the task at hand while keeping thoughts of Gerard from her mind.

Would there ever come a day when thoughts of him didn't fill her head? It had been months since she'd last seen him, but the way her mind persisted in dwelling on him, it might as well have been yesterday.

Distance and time had done nothing to diminish her feelings for him.

GERARD HAD SPENT MUCH TIME OF LATE CONTEMPLATING his feelings for Fern. She had not returned to the Hawks' garden since their last encounter there months ago. He would have sought her out himself, except he didn't know where to find her.

And the only reason why he had not begun another search throughout London was because he suspected that Fern did not wish to be found. Not that he imagined she was trying to hide from him with calculated intent. But if she had wanted to see him, she knew right where he'd be. Her continued absence spoke volumes.

His mother walked into the front parlor just then and launched into a retelling of her recent visit to the milliner's. "You must see the hat I just bought," she announced.

Gerard couldn't care less about some female frippery at the moment—or ever, really—but he pasted on a polite smile for his mother's benefit.

She set a hatbox on the side table and lifted off the lid. "Look at this. Isn't it simply marvelous?" she asked as she pushed aside the wrapping to reveal the hat inside.

She carried on talking about all the special details of "the masterpiece," but Gerard wasn't paying any attention to her words any longer.

He gaze was focused on the name printed on the side of the hatbox. *Fern's Millinery*. He remembered that Fern had mentioned working in a ladies hat shop. Surely, this was too big a coincidence to be mere happenstance.

He intended to find out.

Pushing to his feet, he ignored his mother's sputtering reaction as he exited the room without explanation or apology. A short time later, he reached Fern's Millinery.

He opened the door and stepped inside, immediately becoming the focus of all eyes in the shop. He didn't let that bother him, though, since one lovely pair of blue eyes belonged to his Fern.

"Gerard! I mean, Mr. Hawk," she quickly corrected herself. "What are you doing here?"

"I came to see you. I need to speak with you."

For a moment, she looked as though she intended to refuse, but then she nodded her head. "Come into the back room. We can speak there."

He followed her through the curtained doorway and entered some kind of workroom, where a young girl was stitching a bunch of artificial cherries onto the wide brim of a straw hat.

Fern asked her to assist the customers in the front of the shop, and a moment later, he and Fern were alone.

She turned to face him, her lips parting as she started to speak.

But he didn't give her a chance to get any words out. "I love you, Fern."

Her mouth moved, but no sounds came out in response to his declaration.

Gerard rushed to fill the silence. "I'm sorry for my abruptness, but I feel as though I've spent too much time apart from you already. I don't want to waste another moment. I'd like to court you, if you'll permit."

Still, she remained silent, her eyes wide with surprise.

"You're not a servant any longer—you're the proprietress of your own shop. Although, you must know by now that I would love you and want you no matter what. But surely, the distance between us is not too far to cross any longer?" He paused for a moment to take a deep breath. "Please, Fern. Please. Say something."

"Yes."

"Yes, what? The distance *is* too far to cross?"

"No."

"No, it's not too far? Or no, you won't allow me to court you?" He knew what he wanted her answer to be, but he wasn't going to assume anything, for fear that his hopes might then be crushed.

Her lips curved up in a smile. "I love you, too, Gerard. Does that answer all your questions?"

His breath rushed out in joy and relief, and he gave her his biggest smile. "I believe it does. May I... May I kiss you?"

Again, she said, "Yes." Her eyes bright with happiness.

He leaned down to place a tender kiss on her lips, love and anticipation filling his heart for the future ahead. He intended to shower her with adoration and affection—and a few special gifts, as well.

After all, what was the point of having money if he couldn't share it with the woman he treasured above all else?

The End

THANKS FOR READING

If you **love Victorian Romance**, <u>**Visit Here:**</u>

http://ticahousepublishing.subscribemenow.com

to hear about all <u>**New Faye Godwin Romance Releases!**</u> **I will let you know as soon as they become available!**

Thank you, Friends! If you enjoyed *The Ragged Hatmaker!* would you kindly take a couple minutes to leave a positive review on Amazon? It only takes a moment, and positive reviews truly make a difference. Thank you so much! I appreciate it!

Much love,

Faye Godwin

MORE FAYE GODWIN VICTORIAN ROMANCES!

COMING SOON!

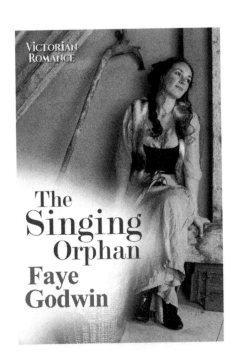

ABOUT THE AUTHOR

Faye Godwin has been fascinated with Victorian Romance since she was a teen. After reading every Victorian Romance in her public library, she decided to start writing them herself —which she's been doing ever since. Faye lives with her husband and young son in England. She loves to travel throughout her country, dreaming up new plots for her romances. She's delighted to join the Tica House Publishing family and looks forward to getting to know her readers.

contact@ticahousepublishing.com